The Fairies FRAN & VERA

This Book Belongs To:

....

Written by
Mama G

Illustrated by
Anouska Sutherland

Fabulous Fran was a fairy.
Vile Vera was one too.
They lived together in Fairy Land;
where dreams seem to come true.

Fabulous Fran does good things:
she loves to make you smile.
While Vera has her wicked ways;
that's why we call her Vile.

Good things come in many forms,
like deeds and open hearts.
And Fran knew this very well,
you see she was fairy smart.

But Vile Vera thought differently,
she wanted the world to be bad.
She wanted it full of hate not love
and wanted to make us mad.

"Coffee?" asked Vera at breakfast.
"Don't mind if I do," said Fran.
"And what have you got to do today?"
"Oh, I've got a plan!"

"A plan?" said Fran. "That can't be good,
what are you up to Vera?"
The coffee poured, our villain implored,
that Fran move a little nearer.

"You know Silly Billy, whose address is:
The Fairlawns, Fairy Land?
He told me something the other day
I'm struggling to understand."

"He's fallen in love!"
"What's wrong with that?"
said Fran, bubbling over with joy.
"Here's the fact: my problem's that
he's fallen in love with a boy."

"A boy? Oh boy! That's wonderful!"
Fran had longed to hear news like this for years.
"But," said Vera with a tut,
"I'm going to make this end in tears.

Everyone knows that love is for
a boy and girl to share,
And by the end of the day, if I have my way,
of this fact he'll be well aware."

"With a wave of my wand,
Billy should see what his life could be."
So Vera gave a quick curse
and Billy landed face first,
amongst their jam and coffee.

Fran screamed. Vera laughed.
Silly Billy's face was in the butter.
"Now to find you the perfect girl."
Not words you want Vera to utter.

A fanfare played and in a glitter haze
Milly came into their life.
"She's pretty," said Billy,
"Yes I am. And I'd be the perfect wife."

"When it comes to looks I'm by the books."
Billy said: "That can't be disputed."
"And what about you, you're handsome too!"
Milly thought she and he were well suited.

But they weren't. For one reason.
Do you know why?
"You'd be my perfect wife, Milly.
If you were a guy."

And as quick as you like,
Milly vanished away, in a puff of smoke.
"Ooh," said Fran, "I tell you what:
I can't wait to meet your bloke!"

But Vile Vera's villainous ways
continued with spells and drama.
Until there appeared (and they were amazed)
a furry, friendly, llama.

"Have you lost your mind?" said
Fran, kindly offering
the llama some tea.

Then through the door
crashed Lily,
"Don't worry she's with me!"

"I'm a llama farmer and this one escaped.
She's got a mind of her own.
Mind you, so have I, they say,
that's why I live alone."

Then to the llama's alarm she was in Lily's arms
and being taken out of the house.
Lily made the llama look so light you thought the
llama might have been a mouse!

"Third time lucky!" Vera cried,
as Fran saw one of her worst fears:
Vile Vera was getting so angry
steam was coming out her ears!

Her face went red, her blood was boiling
and then before they knew it.
She flew into a thousand pieces.
"Oh look," said Fran, "She blew it."

The pieces fell back in to place
and this they thought was strange.
Instead of seeing Vera's face
they saw her rearranged.

"What the what?" Billy exclaimed
and Fran did much the same.
"Are you alright Vera dear?
If indeed Vera's still your name!"

"Of course it's not.
I'm now called Dot!
Do you think you'd
get along with me?"
"Well," said Billy.
"I've always thought:
I could be a friend
of Dorothy's."

Dot looked at Fran askance
and frankly Billy wondered why.
"Is that all I am to him?" she said,
"A friend? I may just cry!"

Fran got a hanky, dabbed Dot's eyes
and said: "Gosh, you are very smart.
But not enough to know why
you've not got Billy's heart."

And Dot howled and Dot wailed
and her tears became a river,
until Dot washed herself away
and all that was left was Vera.

"Enough's enough," said Fran.
"I have to intervene.
Forcing someone to be something
they're not is very VERY mean."

"Billy is a good boy
and he loves a good boy too.
And honestly Vera, who Billy loves
isn't up to you."

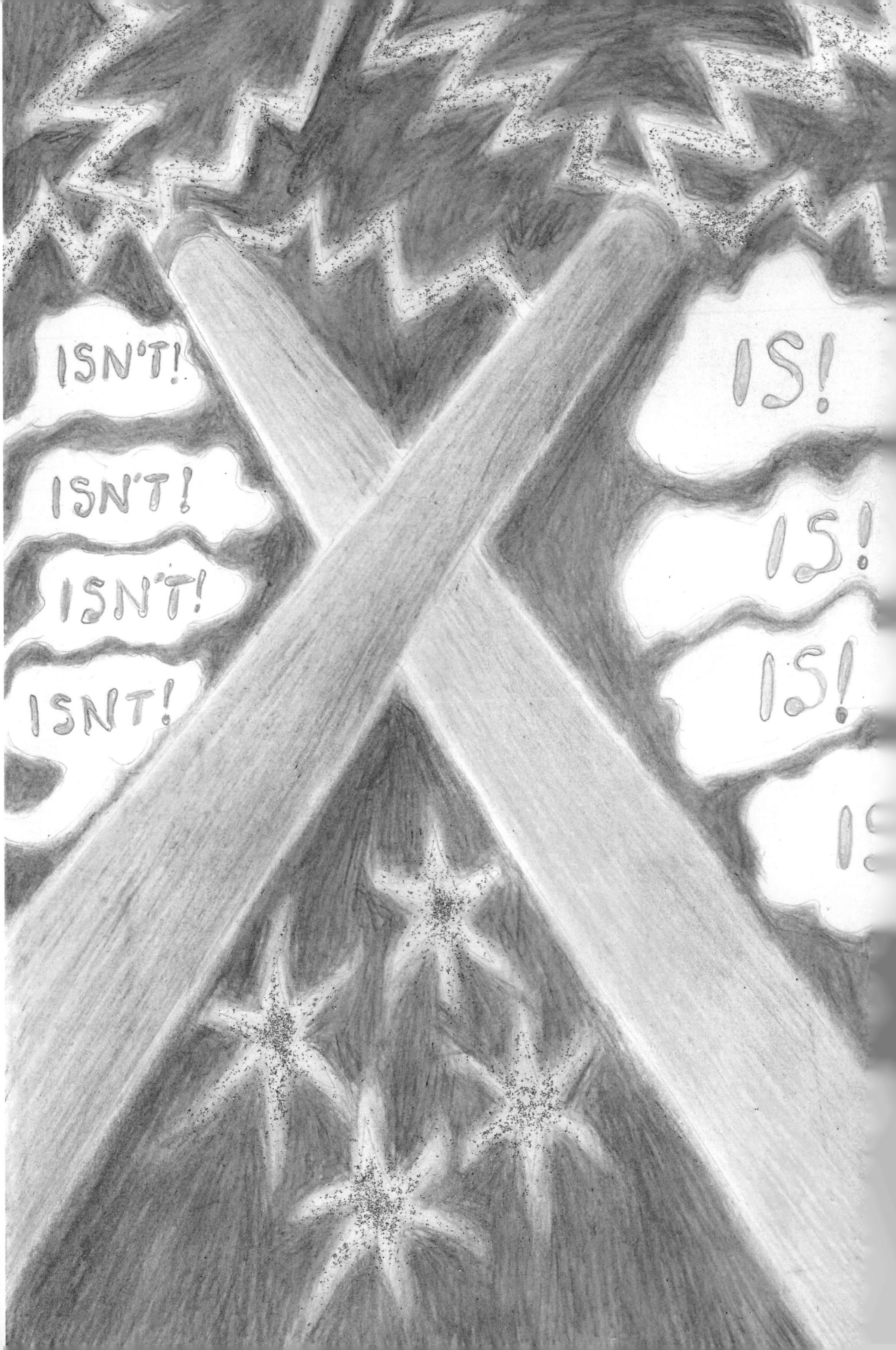
ISN'T!
ISN'T!
ISN'T!
ISNT!
IS!
IS!
IS!

"Oh yes it is!" said Vera,
shooting her wand at Fran.
"Oh no it's not!" Fran said,
shooting her wand right back.

"Is!"

"Isn't!"

"Is!"

"Isn't!"

They were both under attack.

Billy stood there
eyes agog
and gob down
to the floor.
Sparks were flying
around the room.
Who knew what
was in store?

There was a crash
and then a flash and
then a silence fell.
They'd magicked a
man between them.
A man Billy
knew quite well!

He was holding
The Complete Works
of Shakespeare.
To Fran that was
clever and strong.

While Vera just said:
"He's pretty."
And she pretty well
wasn't wrong.

Billy's eyes were
wider than ever
and his smile was
from ear to ear.

"Sam, my love,
it's good to see you;
I'm really glad
you're here!"

They hugged, held hands
and beamed with pride
and for the first time Vera got it:

Love should never have to hide
and no one has the right to stop it.

"Well, I suppose that's one more
at the table for tea."
Said Fran.
Fabulously.

Mama G

Mama G is a panto dame who goes all over the UK (and sometimes Canada!) telling stories about being who you are and loving who you want, to children and their families.

She started telling stories in 2018, the first of which was The Fairies Fran and Vera. Her other characters include hat wearing dinosaurs, flatulent goats, confused horses and a whole host of others, all celebrating our right to be who we are. Mama G has told her stories in schools, nurseries, theatres, bookshops, museums, libraries and at prides and festivals. She's worked with Disney, HSBC, Foyles, Pride in London and Waterstones, to help them share a message of inclusivity with their customers.

During the Coronavirus pandemic, Mama G kept everyone positive with regular live performances on Facebook and Christmas 2020 saw one of her most popular stories Eunice the Horse turned into a magical new musical for families.

To find out more check out @MamaGStories on Facebook, Instagram and YouTube.

Robert Pearce

Robert trained at Rose Bruford College and has been a professional actor since 2005. In that time, he has appeared in over thirty pantomimes, many of which he has written and directed himself, including the annual Haven Holidays summer panto.

Over this time he has worked with some of the UK's most popular performers including Tommy Steele, B*Witched, Union J, Lisa Riley and stars from EastEnders, Neighbours and, perhaps most significantly, 'Allo, 'Allo.

As well as panto, Robert has toured the UK in The Glenn Miller Story, The Wizard of Oz, Charlie and Lola's Best Bestest Play and as Bungle in Rainbow Live!. He's also performed in Shakespeare, Chekhov and a storage container.

Robert has been working closely with Mama G since 2018 and over the years they have become inseparable.

Anouska Sutherland

Anouska Lorraine Sutherland has loved to draw from a very early age. She creates paintings, drawings/ illustrations and collages on a variety of subjects, from her imagination and life.

She studied at Chelsea College of Art & Design and her work has been on display at the Victoria & Albert museum in London, Staff exhibitions: Vamalgam 5, 6 and 7 and at the Art Fayres: We Are Creative in 2018 and 2019 at Lichfield Cathedral, Staffordshire.

She was honoured and delighted to be asked to illustrate her dear friend's 1st book: The Fairies: Fran and Vera by Mama G. She completed the illustrations in Summer Lockdown 2020.

She was born and grew up in the London borough of Hammersmith & Fulham, she is of Jamaican and Grenadian heritage.

She currently lives in Lichfield, Staffordshire with her cat Boudica Louvel.

Printed in Poland
by Amazon Fulfillment
Poland Sp. z o.o., Wrocław

85833994R00021